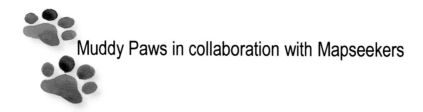 Muddy Paws in collaboration with Mapseekers

Published November 2021

ISBN 978 1 910356 661

© Middleton Press Ltd, 2021
© Muddy Paws Ltd, 2021

Cover design and Design Deborah Esher

Published by
Middleton Press Ltd
126A Camelsdale Road
Haslemere
Surrey
GU27 3RJ
Tel: +44 (0) 01730 813169
Email: info@middletonpress.co.uk
hello@muddypawsbooks.co.uk
www.middletonpress.co.uk
www.muddypaws.co.uk

Printed by
Mapseeker Digital Ltd,
Unit 15, Bridgwater Court
Oldmixon Crescent
Weston Super Mare
North Somerset
BS24 9AY
Tel: +44 (0) 01922 458288 +44 (0) 7947107248

This book is printed on environmentally friendly materials.

This book is dedicated to all those who
believe in unconditional love.

The Magical Land of
Pawsland

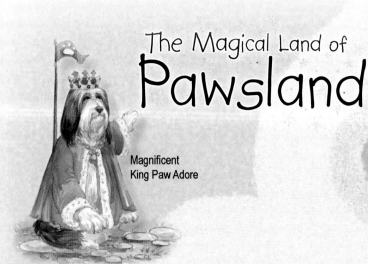

Magnificent
King Paw Adore

N

Tastlybud

Sandypar

Howard's hometown
Bumstill

Howard's
House

W

Hollyberry

The Magical
Pawsland Express

S

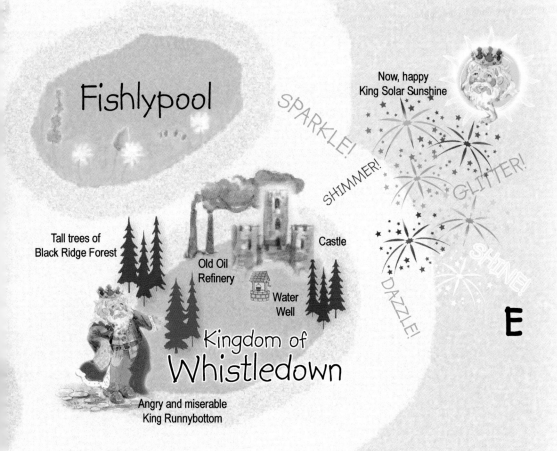

Fishlypool

Now, happy
King Solar Sunshine

SPARKLE!

SHIMMER!

GLITTER!

DAZZLE!

SHINE!

Tall trees of
Black Ridge Forest

Castle

Old Oil
Refinery

Water
Well

Kingdom of
Whistledown

Angry and miserable
King Runnybottom

E

Howard's
big fluffy white paws and
Big Furry Bottom

Pawchester

In a land called Pawsland, in a town called Bumstill, was born the most famous Pawsland pup the world had ever seen...

Howard!

Howard, like all the pups in Pawsland, had enormous fluffy paws and being from the town of Bumstill he had a rather **Big Furry Bottom**. Howard was also gentle and kind.

WAG!

WAG!

WAG!

WAG!

WAG!

You see the job of a Pawsland pup is to spread love and kindness and help show everyone a better way to live.

Howard's
quests were
given to him by
the ruler of Pawsland.

The magnificent
King Paw Adore.

On this day, Howard's
quest was to spread
love and kindness to the
Kingdom of Whistledown.

Word had got to King Paw Adore that
things were not quite as they should be in Whistledown.

The kingdom was beyond the tall trees of the
Black Ridge forest and past the large chimneys of
the old oil refinery.

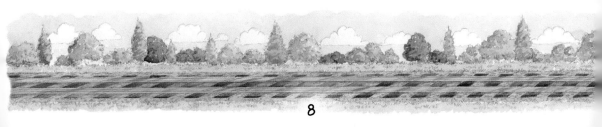

...... on his magical journey to Whistledown

Whistledown
was ruled by the
miserable King Runnybottom,
who had declared that no puppies
were allowed in his Kingdom. They
made people happy, and according to
King Runnybottom that just couldn't happen!

You see, King Runnybottom was always miserable and he thought, if I'm miserable, then everyone else should be miserable too!

...... on his magical journey to Whistledown

In the dark of night, Howard set off on his quest. He raced past the tall trees, and the old oil stack chimneys, on his way to Whistledown.

As Howard approached the town, it was beginning to get light. He could see the big town gates were closed, but he was having trouble being quiet!

Being from Pawsland and having such big fluffy white paws it was difficult for Howard to creep anywhere....

BOOM...
BOOM...
BOOM...

made the noise of Howard's big paws as he reached the town gates.

The noise woke two small children from their beds.

Out of their bedroom window, the children could see Howard approaching. It was obvious that Howard's **Big Furry Bottom** was going to be very difficult to get through the gaps in the locked town gates.

The small boy called Noah and his sister Ivy ran down to help Howard. How they laughed seeing the big furry puppy getting his Big Furry Bottom stuck in the Whistledown town gates.

"If we help you, you won't eat us, will you?" Noah dared to ask, when he saw how big Howard actually was!

"Eat you?" Howard laughed,
"NO, of course not! ..... I'm here to spread love and kindness, and you two children are showing me that right now by coming to help me!
Can you push my Big Furry Bottom through these gates please?"

They all giggled as Howard started jumping and bumping. Noah and Ivy, who were much slimmer than Howard, climbed through the gates and tried to push Howard's Big Furry Bottom through it.

...... on his magical journey to Whistledown

After a short while Howard was free and inside the town of Whistledown, thanks to the help from Noah and Ivy.

Howard thanked
the children
by touching
their heads
gently with
his big furry
soft paws.

...... on his magical journey to Whistledown

Howard explained to Noah and Ivy that he had come to Whistledown to teach King Runnybottom about love and kindness.
"King Runnybottom should let everyone in Whistledown spread love and kindness to each other without fear."

"But the King won't like that!" The children gasped.

"Then take me to your King," said Howard. He wasn't afraid of King Runnybottom, because he knew that love and kindness would always win the day.

As the three approached King Runnybottom's castle they heard a strange sound, a huge rumbling, like bubbling water.

Howard looked at Noah and Ivy, who were rather scared. Noah explained that the people of Whistledown believed the loud noise was King Runnybottom's tummy rumbling, and when it rumbled the King got very angry and miserable indeed!

Howard took another step towards the castle but the children froze.

...... on his magical journey to Whistledown

Howard marched up to the castle
gates and banged
on them with one of his
big fluffy white paws.

BANG...
BANG...
BANG...

"GO AWAY," came a
shout from behind the castle
gates. It was clearly King Runnybottom.

"I'm afraid I can't go away, Your Highness," said Howard
confidently. "I'm Howard of Pawsland and I'm here to
spread love and kindness."

"Well! Make my tummy better then!"

said King Runnybottom.
"Your Highness, if you raise the castle gate maybe
I could come inside and help you?"

Very slowly the castle gate was pulled up and Howard
trotted in to see King Runnybottom, who was bent over
in pain. He had his big gold crown on his head.

Howard approached King Runnybottom and held out one
of his big white fluffy paws. "Your Highness, it's such an
honour to meet you." But the King was in such pain he
could hardly lift his head.

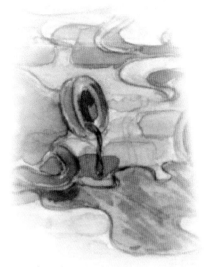

As Howard looked down beside the King, he couldn't help but notice a spilt jug of mucky black water.

"Your Highness, surely you haven't been drinking that dirty water?" he asked worriedly.

"Of course I have,"
              said King Runnybottom.
"It's from the royal well. My parents and all the Kings and Queens before them have always drunk from the well, but, all of a sudden, I'm getting ill!"

"Does the water run down from the mountainside into the well, Your Highness?" asked Howard.

"Yes, I believe it does," replied the King.

"I think your well is being infected by leaking oil from the old refinery on the Black Ridge forest," Howard said.

"Do you mind if I go and check?" Howard asked
                        King Runnybottom.

The King gave his permission
for Howard to go and investigate.

...... on his magical journey to Whistledown

It was clear to Howard that the people of Whistledown, who worked very hard at the oil refinery, had no idea that there was an oil leak infecting the castle well.

"You have to stop NOW!" Howard urged the workmen. Howard told them why he thought the King had been so miserable. "I think it's because the oil's leaking into the King's well and when the King drinks the dirty water, it makes him very ill and gives him a runny bottom."

"But we can't stop now," said the workmen. "If we stop, the town won't have oil for heating or for lighting."

Howard explained to them that the clever puppies of Pawsland use solar panels to collect power from the sun, which can then be used to power the lights and heating in all of Pawsland.

"And you would be kind enough to share your solar panel idea with us?" asked the amazed workmen.

"Of course!" said Howard, smiling. "Our job as Pawsland pups, is to spread love and kindness, and this shows both. It will be much kinder to the planet and much better for the young children of Whistledown to have a cleaner and better future."

Howard ran back to King Runnybottom's castle to tell the King what he had found. He also offered to get help from the people and pups of Pawsland, to change Whistledown from a dirty oil-based town to a clean solar powered town.

The King was so pleased with Howard's findings and ideas. **He ordered the changes to take place immediately.**

.... In no time at all, King Runnybottom felt better because his drinking water was now clean. He wanted to celebrate this monumental change for the Kingdom.

He declared that there should be **a huge party in Whistledown,** with balloons, wonderful food and a fantastic firework display! Very cleverly, the King made sure the fireworks had no bangs, just beautiful bright colours, so as not to scare any animals. Howard was given a place at the King's table for the party and he invited Noah and Ivy as his guests.
King Runnybottom then announced,

"I shall now be known as
King Solar Sunshine,
as I feel happy and well once again ....

.... Whistledown,
no longer has a runny-bottomed King!"
Everyone cheered .... "Hooray!"

The King then declared that all puppies were welcome in his Kingdom, and should always be treated with love and kindness.

When the party was all over, the whole of Whistledown came out to wave Howard goodbye, including, King Solar Sunshine, Noah and Ivy.

As Howard turned to walk away, as if like magic, a fabulous train appeared to take him home. Howard knew the train had been sent by the magnificent King Paw Adore of Pawsland. It was indeed the magical Pawsland Express. Howard climbed aboard and in a flash was disappearing into the distance, homeward bound to prepare for his next exciting adventure ....

...... on his magical journey to Whistledown

As Howard waved to the children he shouted,

"Look out for my next adventure. I'll tell you all about the magical Pawsland Express and how it's fuelled to help keep our beautiful land clean and healthy!"

...... on his magical journey to Whistledown

Memjoa Photography

Howard with his owner, author, Mark Taylor

Dogs come into our lives for many different reasons,
but they all bring unconditional love.

"Howard brought a love so powerful it helped me through the most challenging moments in my life. He inspired me to write about him in a way that would help children realise love and kindness should always be the way forward and if I can somehow plant the seed of sustainability into a child's mind at the same time, then I will have done Howard's love justice."

When Mark approached Middleton Press, and discussed publishing his *Howard of Pawsland* book, he was told "we only publish railway books", hence the "Pawsland Express" came about, and "Muddy Paws Books" was formed.

H**oward** **on his magical** **2**
of Pawsland **train journey to**
Tastlybud

find out about The Pawsland Express and its sustainable fuel.

Howard **saves** **3**
of Pawsland **Fishlypool**

see how Howard solves the fishermen's problems.

Howard **and his** **4**
of Pawsland **adventure with**
Pawchester United

can Howard save the Pawchester football pitch?